Steadwell Books World Tour
NIGERIA

PATRICK DALEY

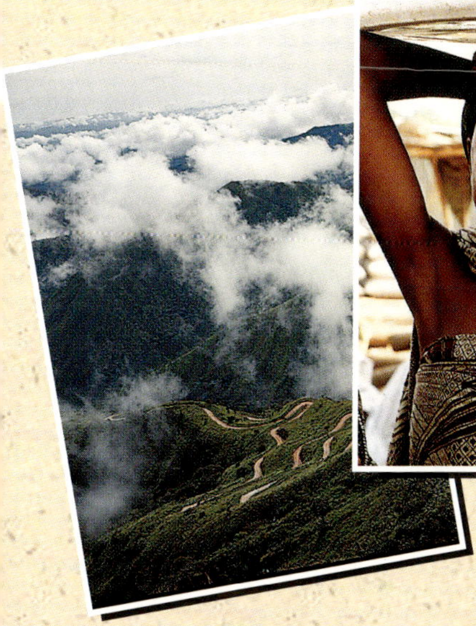

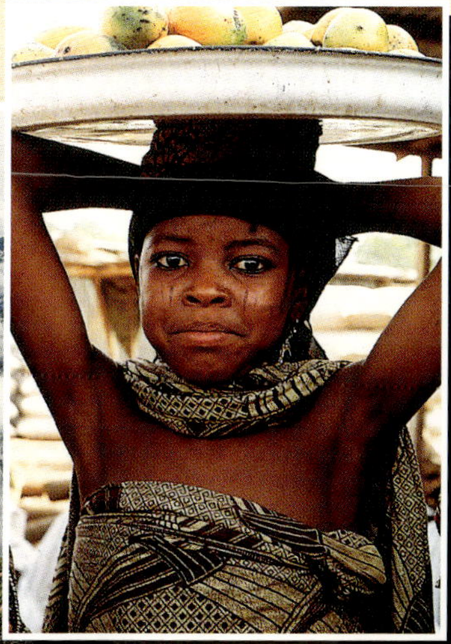

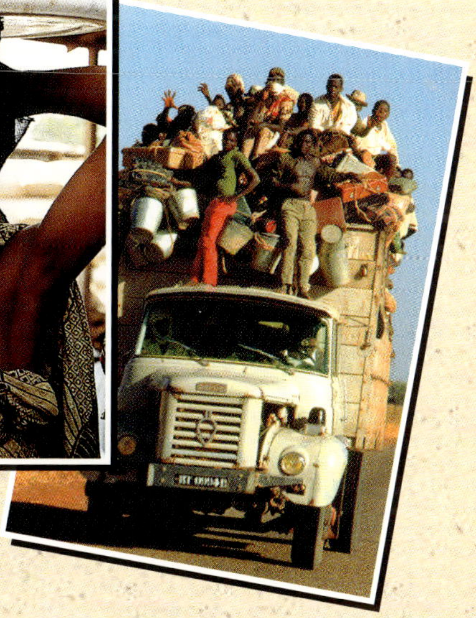

Raintree Steck-Vaughn Publishers
A Harcourt Company

Austin · New York
www.raintreesteckvaughn.com

Copyright © 2002 Steck-Vaughn Company

All rights reserved. No part of this book may be reproduced or utilized in any form or by any means, electronic or mechanical, including photocopying, recording, or by any information storage and retrieval system, without permission in writing from the publisher. Inquiries should be addressed to: Copyright Permissions, Steck-Vaughn Company, P.O. Box 26015, Austin, TX 78755.

Published by Raintree Steck-Vaughn Publishers,
an imprint of Steck-Vaughn Company

Editor: Simone T. Ribke
Designer: Maria E. Torres

Library of Congress Cataloging-in-Publication Data
Daley, Patrick.
   Nigeria / Patrick Daley.
      p. cm. -- (Steadwell books world tour)
   Includes bibliographical references and index.
   Summary: Describes the country of Nigeria, including information on its history, geography, government, economy, religion, social life and customs, and some popular tourist sites.
   ISBN 0-7398-4713-9
      1. Nigeria--Juvenile literature. [1. Nigeria.] I. Title. II. Series.

DT515.22 .D35 2002
966.9--dc21   2001048958

Printed in the United States of America
10 9 8 7 6 5 4 3 2 1 W 05 04 03 02

Photo acknowledgments
Cover (a) ©Victor Englebert/Englebert Photography; cover (b) ©Jason Lauré; cover(c) ©Zefa/H. Armstrong Roberts; p.1a ©Zefa/H. Armstrong Roberts; p.1b ©Jason Lauré; p.1c ©Victor Englebert/Englebert Photography; p.3a ©Jason Lauré; p.3b ©Zefa/H. Armstrong Roberts; p.5 ©Trip/J. Mason; p.6 ©British Museum, London/Bridgeman Art Library, London/SuperStock; p.7 ©Jason Lauré; p.8 ©George Esiri/Reuters/Getty Images; p.13 ©Wolfgang Kaehler/CORBIS; p.14 ©SuperStock; p.15 ©Wolfgang Kaehler/CORBIS; p.16 ©Jason Lauré; p.19 ©Daniel Aubry; p.20 ©Victor Englebert/Englebert Photography; p.21a ©Paul Almasy/CORBIS; p.21b ©TRIP/Viesti Collection; p.22 ©M.P. Kahl/DRK Photo; p.23 ©Animals Animals; p.24 ©Trip/J. Highet; p.25 ©Trip/J. Highet; p.26 ©Brennan Linsley/AP/Wide World Photos; p.27a ©Trip/J. Hightet; p.27 b ©Jason Lauré; p.28 ©Trip/G Warne; p.29 ©Stuart Milligan/Allsport; p. 31a ©Bruce Coleman; p.31b ©Eric Miller/Jason Lauré; p.33 ©Daniel Aubry; p.34 ©Bruce Coleman; p.35 ©Jason Lauré; p.37 ©Margaret Courtney-Clarke/CORBIS; p.38 ©Clement Ntaye/AP/Wide World Photos; p.39 ©Eric Miller/Jason Lauré; p.40 ©AFP/CORBIS; p.41 ©Ben Radford/Allsport; p.42 ©Daniel Aubry; p.43a ©Wolfgang Kaehler/CORBIS; p.43b ©Jason Lauré; p.44a ©Pelletier Micheline/CORBIS SYGMA; p.44b ©Otto Greule/Allsport; p.44c ©Trip/J. Highet.

Additional photography by Steck-Vaughn Collection.

J
966.9
DAL

CONTENTS

Nigeria's Past 6
A Look at Nigeria's Geography 10
Lagos: A Big-City Snapshot 16
4 Top Sights 20
Going to School in Nigeria 28
Nigerian Sports 29
From Farming to Factories 30
Nigerian Government 32
Religions of Nigeria 33
Nigerian Food 34
Cookbook 35
Up Close: The Niger Delta 36
Holidays 40
Learning the Language 41
Quick Facts 42
People to Know 44
More to Read 45
Glossary 46
Index 48

Welcome to Nigeria

Are you planning a trip to Nigeria? Maybe you want to know a little more about this great country. Or perhaps you just like reading about ancient ruins, life in river villages, and fast-paced shopping markets. Whatever the reason is for picking up this book, you are in for a treat. Nigeria is a county with a fascinating history. It has an incredible landscape and plenty of interesting people.

A Tip as You Get Started

• *Use the Table of Contents*

It can be helpful to know what topics will be covered. Take a look at the previous page, called "Contents." There, you can pick the chapters that interest you and start with those. You can always check out the other chapters later.

• *Use the Index*

If you need to find information on a very specific topic, turn to the "Index." It is found at the back of the book. The Index lists many of the subjects covered in the book. It will tell you what pages to find them on.

• *Use the Glossary*

As you read this book, you may notice that some words appear in **bold** print. Look up bold words in the Glossary. The Glossary will help you learn what they mean. It is found on page 46.

▲ JOS PLATEAU
This beautiful grassland is located in the middle of Nigeria. It covers 5,100 square miles (13,300 sq km). It is home to exotic bats, small antelope, and brightly colored birds.

NIGERIA'S PAST

Nigeria is a country with a very exciting history. Learning about its past is the key to understanding the present Nigeria. Many Nigerians had ancestors in the area 40,000 years ago. That's right—the history of Nigeria is over 40,000 years old! Also, there are over 250 different groups of people living in this country! So what does this mean? It means there are a lot of different stories to tell.

Ancient History

The earliest Nigerian people were the Nok civilization. They lived on the Jos Plateau nearly 2,500 years ago. The Nok civilization is best known for its cool clay sculptures.

The next major empires that we know of were the Kanem-Bornu kingdom, the Hausa, the Yoruba, and the kingdom of Benin. They formed between A.D. 800 and A.D. 1300. The Kanem-Bornu kingdom started in the country of Chad. They became the largest, most powerful group of people in Nigeria by the year 1000.

The Hausa settled to the west of the Kanem-Bornu kingdom. They were known as traders and merchants. Today, the Hausa people are still known for this. The Hausa language is an important business language in

◀ **BENIN CULTURE ARTIFACT**
The kingdom of Benin flourished between the 15th and 17th centuries. It was well known for its brass and ivory sculptures.

▶ **THE HAUSA PEOPLE**
The Hausa have inhabited the north since the 14th century. They were great traders and merchants. Right, three Hausa children pose with their helpful donkey.

Africa. The Yoruba people controlled southern Nigeria. Their capital was the city Ife, near Lagos. The Yoruba were famous for their beautiful art. They prospered well into the 19th century. The kingdom of Benin stood to the east of Ife and the Yoruba. The Benin people used the Niger River to trade with other peoples. Benin flourished between the 15th and 17th centuries and became well known for its brass and ivory sculptures.

European Empires

In the 14th century, the first Europeans arrived and started an international slave trade. During this period over 20 million people left Africa as slaves! Europeans were not the first to enslave Africans. Slavery already existed between tribes and could be just as brutal.

Eventually, the British took control of Nigeria. In 1807 the British outlawed slavery. The British brought useful things to Nigeria like farming techniques and trade. However, they took Nigeria's independence.

▲ **TROUBLED TIMES**
Nigerian soldiers guard homes destroyed by riots in Warri, Nigeria, in 1999. Although its ten-year civil war ended in 1970, Nigeria continues to experience periods of violence and unrest.

Recent History

In 1960 the British left Nigeria. So what happened next? Unfortunately, Nigeria's recent history has seen many difficulties.

B.C. 8000 7000 6000 5000 4000 3000 2000 1000 0

499 B.C.
Nok civilization
lived on the
Jos Plateau.

Nigeria gained independence in 1960. However, there was a huge power struggle. Different peoples in Nigeria could not agree on a form of government. They also fought over who should be in charge. From 1960 to 1970, Nigeria underwent a period of violent civil war. This took place mainly between the Igbo in the south and the Hausa in the north. Each side was afraid the other had too much power. Thousands of people died during this period.

In 1970, the civil wars ended. Nigerians attempted to put together a more unified government. Since then, different peoples in Nigeria have worked together better than they did before 1970. Still, there have been some periods of unrest.

In the past few years, Nigeria has tried very hard to keep away from this violence. For the first time in many years, Nigeria has a civilian leader. This is someone who was elected by the people—not someone who took power by force. His name is President Olusegun Obasanjo. Many think he will help Nigeria to fight less. Some people are doubtful that Nigeria has left its troubles behind. Most people, however, see a bright future for this country.

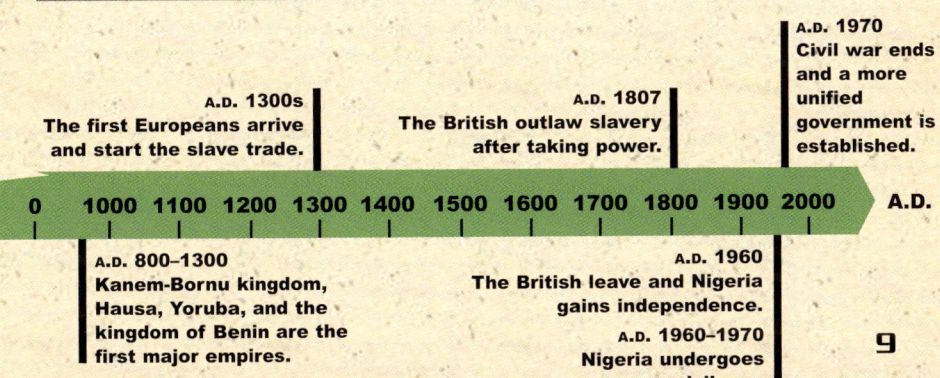

A Look at Nigeria's Geography

If this is your first trip to Nigeria, then you will probably want to see everything. Well, that is going to be hard. There are **rain forests**, deserts, savannas, **swampland**, and beaches. With so much to choose from, it might be hard to decide where to start.

Land

Nigeria is quite big. It is about the size of the state of Texas. Beautiful beaches line Nigeria's coast. They have palm trees, white sand, and huge breaking waves. They are pretty deserted. That means there are very few boardwalks, bumper cars, or jet-ski rentals.

Farther in from the coast, Nigeria is covered with mangrove swamps. (The mangrove is a kind of tree with exposed roots. It grows very well near water.) North of the mangrove swamps sits a **dense** forest. Even farther north is savanna. A savanna is land covered with tall grasses and sparse woodlands.

If you keep heading north, you will reach the Jos Plateau. This huge, flat **plain** covers nearly 3,000 square miles (4,828 sq km). It rises 5,000 feet (1,524 m) above **sea level**. It is dry. Its vegetation, or plant life, is sparse. Dimlang Peak is the highest point in Nigeria. It lies in the eastern Uplands. It measures 6,699 feet (2,042 m) above sea level.

▶ **NIGERIA'S SIZE**
Nigeria has an area of 356,669 square miles (923,768 sq km). It borders four countries: Niger, Benin, Cameroon, and Chad. The Atlantic Ocean lies along its south coast.

11

Water

Did you ever wonder how Nigeria got its name? Take a look at the map, below—see the river that runs through it? This river is called the Niger. It is one of the longest rivers in the world. It stretches 2,600 miles (4,184 km). However, much of this river lies in the countries to the north. Other important rivers in Nigeria include the Benue and the Kaduna.

Nigeria's southern coast lies on the Gulf of Guinea. This is part of the Atlantic Ocean. Nigeria also borders a huge body of water to the northeast called Lake Chad. During the rainy season, Lake Chad swells to 30,000 square feet (78,000 sq km). In the south, the Niger River spreads out as it meets the Atlantic Ocean. This area is called the Niger **Delta.**

▲ **NIGER RIVER**
The Niger is one of the longest rivers in the world. It provides water, food, and transportation to many Nigerians.

◀ **BEATING THE HEAT**
Nigeria can get hot, hot, hot! Left, a woman uses an umbrella to shade herself against the scorching sun. She is shopping in an open-air market in Ibadan.

Weather

Nigeria is a tropical country. That means it is hot all year long. In the coastal areas, the temperature averages about 80 degrees Fahrenheit (27° C). Inland, average temperatures rise above 90 degrees Fahrenheit (32° C). It gets a little cooler in Nigeria's high elevations. So if you are feeling too hot and sweaty, head to the mountains.

The southern forests and swampland receive huge amounts of rain. Over 100 inches (254 cm) fall each year. Farther north, it is drier. The average rainfall there is about 25 inches (64 cm) per year.

One amazing feature of Nigeria's weather is a wind called the harmattan. In the winter months, this dry, hot wind blows south from the Sahara Desert. It brings a coating of fine sand to Nigeria's northern regions. If you hear a harmattan is coming, head inside. Otherwise you will be picking sand out of your ears for months!

▲ NIGERIAN SANDSTORM
Sandstorms occur often during the winter months. They are caused by the harmattan. The harmattan is a strong, hot wind that blows sand from the Sahara Desert.

LAGOS: A BIG-CITY SNAPSHOT

▲ **LAGOS ISLAND**
Lagos Island is located in the middle of the city of Lagos. The downtown area is very modern. It has many tall buildings and shopping centers.

Lagos is Africa's largest **metropolis**. Over 14 million people live there. The city covers about 77 square miles (200 sq km) and spreads across three islands.

Lagos Island

Four main areas make up Lagos. The most important (and most lively) of these is Lagos Island. Lagos Island lies in the middle of Lagos. It is home to countless skyscrapers and shopping areas. It has long strips of expensive restaurants and an exciting nightlife.

If you're in the mood to shop, the first place you should check out is Broad Street. Later, head to the Brazilian Quarter. Many Brazilian slaves returned to Nigeria after they were freed. They built their homes and businesses in this area.

Another important destination on Lagos Island is Nigeria's National Museum. Many people say that "Treasures of Ancient Nigeria" is the best exhibit. Some of this Nigerian art is 2,500 years old.

Victoria Island

Victoria Island is another major district. Victoria Island is filled with mansions, businesses, and the **embassies** of foreign countries.

For a look at daily life on Victoria Island, head to the Bar Beach Market. You can pick up supplies for a picnic, get your shoes fixed, or buy some presents for your friends.

Ikoyi Island

Ikoyi Island is the third "must-see" island in Lagos. It has a vibrant nightlife. The center of the Ikoyi scene is Awolowo Road. The Falomo Shopping Center has some of the best dyed fabric in Nigeria. Batik is the name for this special fabric. Batik is multicolored and covered with cool designs.

The Mainland

The Mainland is the biggest part of Lagos. It is home to the University of Lagos, Murtala Muhammed **International** Airport, and the National Stadium. It is also where Lagos's **inhabitants** live. Unlike the rest of Lagos, most of the people here live in terrible **poverty**. Miles and miles of makeshift villages called **shanties** fill this area.

The National Theater hosts Nigeria's important plays and musical events. The Center for Black and African Arts and Civilization is found there. It contains a huge library and museum. There is an exciting gallery for modern Nigerian arts and crafts. You can even check out how batik fabric is made.

LAGO'S TOP-10 CHECKLIST

Confused by all the cool things to do? Here's a list of Lagos's top sights.

- ☐ Head to Broad Street and buy some new clothes.
- ☐ Wander around the Brazilian Quarter and check out neat buildings.
- ☐ Go to the National Museum and freshen up on your Nigerian history.
- ☐ At the National Museum, step back in time at the "Treasures of Ancient Nigeria" exhibit.
- ☐ Take a tour of the Eleke Crescent. See how the rich and famous live.
- ☐ Buy lunch and a new pair of sandals at Bar Beach Market.
- ☐ Browse the fancy boutiques on Awolowo Road.
- ☐ Head to the Falomo Shopping Center to buy batiks.
- ☐ Catch a play at the National Theater.
- ☐ Head to the National Theater's arts and crafts section. See how batiks are made.

▲ **NATIONAL THEATER**
This cultural center in Lagos has a lot to offer. It hosts plays and musical performances. There is also a huge library and a museum with Nigerian arts and crafts.

4 TOP SIGHTS

With so many places to visit, you will need a way to get around. You can travel Nigeria-style in a bush taxi. A bush taxi is a small bus or van that whips people around the country. It can go through the bush, the African term for wilderness. Bush taxis have schedules, but no one follows them. They leave when they are full. That means you can be on time and the taxi has already left. Or it can mean that you will have to wait three days for the next taxi to leave.

What happens if the bush taxi is too full? No problem! The driver will ask extra passengers to sit on the roof. Getting places is half the fun—especially if you are on the roof of a bush taxi.

Kano

The most important area in Kano is the "old city." The first thing to see is the old city gates. They used to protect Kano from invaders. They are all that is left of the famous wall that surrounded this walled city.

Next, check out the Emir's palace. The Emir is Kano's **traditional leader**. Even if you do not get in, the Emir's palace is quite a sight from the outside.

Then explore Kurmi Market. Often what is labeled as an **antique** is really brand new. The best things to buy are clothes. These fabrics are made right around the corner in the dye pits. Head to the dye pits to see how they are made. Warning: Do not stand too close to the edge!

▶ **BUSH TAXIS**
The bush taxi is one way to get around in Nigeria. If it's full, passengers just climb on top—and hold on tight.

▼ CENTRAL MOSQUE OF KANO

The Central Mosque is found within Kano's ancient walls. The Hausa built the walls 1,000 years ago. The mosque is closed to non-Islamic visitors. But it is worth a visit. Every Friday, up to 50,000 worshipers gather for prayer.

▶ KURMI MARKET

This woman sells brightly colored fabrics at the Kurmi market in Kano. The fabrics are dyed right around the corner in dye pits. They make a great souvenir!

Gashaka Gumpti National Park

While in Nigeria, you'll want to meet some wild animals. Head to the Gashaka Gumpti National Park. This is Nigeria's largest national park. It covers over 37,000 square miles (7,000 sq km). It contains mountains, rivers, and enormous savannas.

Gashaka Gumpti National Park has many native wild animals. There are plenty of chimpanzees, elephants, and hippopotami. Gashaka Gumpti is home to rarer kinds of animals, as well. These include leopards, lions, and giant forest pigs. Are these animals dangerous? Definitely. And they will eat you.

▲ HAKUNA MATATA?
Warthogs, like this giant forest hog, are not quite as friendly as in the movies. But they do enjoy wallowing in the mud. Mud helps them stay cool in the daytime heat.

▼ HAPPY HIPPOS
They spend their day snoozing in the water. At night, they come out to graze on land. "Hippopotamus" means "river horse."

FASCINATING FACT
A hippopotamus may seem friendly. But BE CAREFUL! Hippos cause more human deaths than any other animal in Africa. Hippos have no natural enemies. But they are afraid people will hurt them, just the same. Hippopotami become very fierce if they feel threatened.

The Sacred Forest

Nigeria is home to people of many different religions. While you are there, visit some **shrines** and religious sites. A truly amazing spot to visit is the Sacred Forest.

The Sacred Forest is just outside the city of Oshogbo. It is in the south. Mostly Yoruba people live there. In fact, the Sacred Forest is a Yoruba religious site. It is home to countless shrines of Yoruba gods. The forest itself is dedicated to the female goddess of water.

The shrines are extremely old. Today, a European artist named Suzanne Wegner works to fix them up. She makes sure that the shrines are kept in good condition. That way, people can visit and enjoy them for many years to come.

▲ **TRADITIONAL YORUBA MUSICIANS**
These musicians are Yoruba drummers. They are dressed in traditional Yoruba clothing.

▲ TREE ROOT SCULPTURE
This sculpture sits outside the Ojubo Oshun Shrine. It is found in the Sacred Forest. It is a religious site for the Yoruba people.

Tarkwa Beach

If you are looking to relax, you might like to swim in the ocean. Where is the best place to do this? Most Nigerians will tell you the same thing: Tarkwa Beach.

This beautiful beach area is close to Lagos, Nigeria's largest city. You need to take a ferry to get there. It is a tropical paradise. There is white sand, tall palm trees, and calm water. Tarkwa is a great swimming beach because there is no **current**. The currents on other Nigerian beaches can be too strong to make swimming safe.

Some say that Tarkwa Beach is too crowded. Others think the crowds are what make it great. If you want to check out Nigerian people having a blast, this is the place to be. It is a great way to meet some new Nigerian friends. You can also build a giant sand castle or search for cool seashells. It is the beach, after all!

▲ **TARKWA BEACH AT SUNSET**
Tarkwa Beach is a tropical paradise. There is no current, so the water is very calm. This makes it a great place to swim.

▶ **HANDMADE BASKETS**
Nigerian crafts, like these handmade baskets, make good souvenirs. They can be purchased at markets in Lagos and other centers.

▼ **HOW MUCH?**
An Ibo woman bargains at a street market near Tarkwa Beach. Street market vendors sell food, clothing, and many other items.

GOING TO SCHOOL IN NIGERIA

Want to learn how to hunt deer? Dying to take up goat farming? Feeling the need to brush up on your weaving? Then Nigerian bush school may be the place for you. "Bush" is a term that means backcountry or wilderness. Bush schools teach the skills needed to live in the bush environment. These schools are located across the Nigerian countryside.

Nigeria also has schools like you find everywhere else in the world. The students all have to wear uniforms. They are required to take classes in one of the regional languages. The most widely spoken languages are Ibo, Hausa, and Yoruba. These schools also start to teach English when students are about 9 years old.

▲ A NIGERIAN CLASSROOM
Nigerian students study in the language spoken in their regions. Ibo, Hausa, and Yoruba are the most widespread languages. Many children begin to learn English at age 9.

NIGERIAN SPORTS

Ask Nigerians what the most popular sport in Nigeria is. They will always give you the same answer—soccer! They will also tell you the name of the world's best soccer team—the Nigerian Super Eagles. In 1996, their soccer team won an Olympic gold medal. That is something many countries only dream about.

Nigerians are also crazy about their local teams. Most big cities have their own soccer team and a large public stadium.

Nigerians like other sports, as well. In the north, camel racing is very popular. In the south they race canoes. Once a year, on the Sokoto River, they hold a huge fishing contest. Whoever catches the most fish wins.

▶ **CAMEL RACES**
In this sport, jockeys ride dromedary camels—the kind with only one hump. Racing camels have smaller humps. They are very lean. Some run as fast as 23 mph (37 kph).

FROM FARMING TO FACTORIES

Over half the people in Nigeria are farmers. You would probably recognize their main **crops**. Chances are, you have eaten them and thought they were delicious.

Nigeria produces much of the world's kola nuts and cacao. Kola nuts are the main ingredient in (surprise!) cola. Every time you have a cola soft drink, you are drinking kola nuts. The cacao plant produces cocoa beans, the main ingredient in chocolate.

Nigeria's most important crops are yams (a long root vegetable), rice, and corn. Nigerians also grow lots and lots of peanuts. They are one of the favorite foods of Nigerian people. Peanuts are also something farmers sell for cash. When a crop is sold, farmers get paid in naira, which is the Nigerian **currency**.

Another large business in Nigeria is oil production. Nigeria has huge oil reserves. An oil reserve is a pocket of oil located deep in the earth. Nigerians build deep wells into the oil reserves. The wells bring the oil to the surface. Some wells are on the land. Others are built on platforms on the water.

The oil industry is extremely important to the Nigerian economy because it employs so many people. Nigeria sells its oil to countries around the world. Almost 95% of Nigeria's money comes from oil sales.

Many Nigerians also make a living fishing. After all, Nigeria does have a huge coastline. Fishing villages are spread along Nigeria's shores.

▲ KOLA NUTS
Do you like cola soft drinks? If so, you have Nigeria to thank. That's because Nigeria produces most of the world's kola nuts—the main ingredient in cola soft drinks.

◀ DRILLING FOR OIL ON THE NIGER DELTA
Nigeria produces a lot of oil. Many Nigerians work in this industry. Oil is a very important resource. It is used to fuel cars and make electricity.

THE NIGERIAN GOVERNMENT

The Nigerian government consists of a president, a Senate, and a House of Representatives. It is a democracy. That means the people have a say in how the government runs. They vote to elect officials to represent them in each branch of government.

The president's **term** in office lasts for four years. A president can serve only two terms of office. The current president is named Olusegun Obasanjo. He is dedicated to keeping the peace in Nigeria, and he wants to make sure that people keep their freedoms.

There are 360 members of the House of Representatives and 109 members of the Senate. Terms for both of these branches of government last for four years.

Abuja is the capital of Nigeria. The central government is located there. Nigeria also has state and local governments. The local, state, and central governments share power, and each must answer to the people at election time.

NIGERIA'S NATIONAL FLAG

The Nigerian flag has three large stripes, or panels. There are two green panels on the sides. There is one white panel in the middle. The green color represents agriculture, or farming. The white stands for peace and unity.

RELIGIONS OF NIGERIA

Islam is the most widespread religion in Nigeria. Almost half of all Nigerians are Muslims—followers of Islam. Muslims follow the teachings of a man named Muhammad. These are found in a holy book called the Koran.

Mosques are Muslim temples. You can see them in almost every Nigerian city. How can you find a city's mosque? Usually it is the nicest building in town. Look for the towers, called minarets, that surround the mosque. People read prayers from them.

Christians make up more than one-third of Nigerian people. Christianity is found mostly in the south, where the Yoruba people live. Some are Catholics. Christians observe the teachings of Jesus as written in the New Testament of the Bible.

The rest of Nigeria practices traditional religions. They worship different gods and goddesses. If you head to the Sacred Forest near Oshogbo, you can experience traditional Nigerian religion. One of the most important Yoruba goddesses is Onkoro, the mother goddess. She has a shrine in the Sacred Forest that is 15 feet (4.6 m) high.

▶ GREAT MOSQUE IN NIGERIA'S CAPITAL, ABUJA
Muslims, followers of Islam, worship together in buildings called mosques. Almost 50% of all Nigerians are Muslim.

33

NIGERIAN FOOD

Soup or stew is probably the most popular type of meal in Nigeria. It is usually pretty thick, with many ingredients—grains, vegetables, meats, and lots of hot spices. (Nigerians use tons of chilies in their cooking, so be careful.) The most popular kinds of soup are yam soup, palm nut soup, and fish soup.

What is the coolest thing about Nigerian soup? You get to eat it with your fingers! Just make a little cup with your right hand (never your left!) and dig in.

Nigeria is also famous for its snack foods. You can buy snacks at stands in cities and towns all over Nigeria. Nigerians love peanuts—roasted and salted. They also eat plenty of fried cakes and breads. Another favorite snack is the Nigerian version of potato chips—yam chips. The yam is a lot like a sweet potato.

In some markets you can also buy camel meat, rat meat, or a bucket of snails. What more could you possibly want?

◀ **A PAIL OF SNAILS**
Snails are one exotic food you can try in Nigeria. They are sold in buckets at local markets. Believe it or not, snails are considered a delicacy in many parts of the world.

COOKBOOK

Nigerian Recipe

PUFF-PUFF RECIPE

Makes 40-60 Puff-Puffs
2 cups flour
2 cups water
1 cup sugar
2 tsp yeast
Vegetable oil for deep frying
Powdered sugar for topping

WARNING:
Never cook or bake by yourself. Always have an adult assist you in the kitchen.

Directions:
Combine the flour, sugar, water, and yeast together until you have a smooth batter. Let the batter sit for about two hours to rise. Heat the oil in a deep frying pan on low heat.

Test the oil by putting a drop of the batter into the hot oil. If the oil is hot enough, the batter will rise to the top and the oil will bubble slightly. When the oil is hot enough, use a large spoon to drop the batter into the oil in small spoonfuls. Be careful not to burn yourself by splashing the oil. Let the batter drop in gently. Fry the batter until it is golden brown. Turn it as needed.

When the puff-puffs are golden brown, remove them from the oil. Place on a plate with paper towels to drain.

Finally, roll the puff-puffs in the powdered sugar and enjoy.

UP CLOSE: THE NIGER DELTA

The Niger River is one of the longest rivers in the world. It is over 2,600 miles (4,184 km) long. At the end of the river is one of the world's largest deltas. It is about 14,000 square miles (36,260 sq km) and is the biggest river delta in Africa. This delta is home to many types of animals and plant life—water snakes, parrots, mangroves, and so on. Nigeria's largest oil and **mineral deposits** are also found in the delta.

Port Harcourt

The biggest city in the delta is Port Harcourt. It is a booming oil town smack in the middle of a rain forest. It is called the garden city because there are plants, trees, and flowers everywhere. It is a great place to rest up, catch a movie, or go out to eat.

Need some transportation? Water taxis head off in every direction. Helicopters hop from town to town. Oil workers need the helicopters to get around. Sometimes they will let you come along, but they will be sure to charge you hefty fees.

Off to the Islands

Brass Island is a neat place to hang out. The most interesting thing about Brass Island is the strange way some of the locals dress. They wear clothes you would find in Europe 150 years ago. These fashions came into style when the British ruled this area. When the British left, their clothing style mysteriously stayed popular. Do not be surprised to see men in bow ties and top hats walking by.

▲ WATER TAXI ON THE NIGER DELTA

The delta's swampy mangrove forests and sandy wetlands make it hard to get to. Bush taxis are not exactly equipped for this kind of trip. The best way to get around the delta is by water taxi—it works like a bush taxi, except in water. Water taxis will take you wherever you want to go. They will give you a great view of the delta along the way.

Problems with Big Oil

Oil has made the Niger Delta one of Nigeria's richest areas. However, the oil industry causes problems for the locals. Often whole villages have been moved to make way for oil companies. The Saro people in this region have been victims of such development. When they have tried to resist, the government has met them with violence. The most famous example of this is the **execution** of Ken Saro-Wiwa. He was one of Nigeria's most important writers.

Ken Saro-Wiwa protested Nigeria's oil development. In 1995, the Nigerian government executed him for this. The world was outraged that the Nigerian government punished someone for speaking freely about his feelings and opinions. The world demanded that the Nigerian government stop its crackdown on **free speech**. Since Saro-Wiwa's execution, things in Nigeria have improved. With President Obasanjo's election, people hope that the Niger Delta's oil problems will be solved peacefully.

◀ **OIL PIPELINE DISASTER**
A girl flees after an oil pipeline explodes in 2000. The explosion killed more than 100 villagers along th Niger Delta.

◀ **PORT HARCOURT**
Right, an oil tanker docks at Port Harcourt. The oil industry thrives here. But residents of the Niger Delta know it brings problems as well as jobs and money.

▲ **DANGERS CAUSED BY THE OIL INDUSTRY**
Gas flares up at an oil facility in Ogoniland. Oil production is dangerous to the people and the environment along the Niger Delta.

HOLIDAYS

Nigerians observe many national and religious holidays. One important holiday is National Day. It is on October 1 and there is lots of celebrating, flag-waving, and dancing.

Christian and Muslim holidays are very important in Nigeria. One important Christian holiday is Christmas. It marks the birth of Jesus and falls on December 25. If you like parties, then you will love Christmas in Nigeria. There are big celebrations and drumming contests.

For Muslims, a very sacred time is Ramadan. It lasts for one month. Ramadan falls in the ninth month of the Muslim calendar year. During Ramadan, Muslims **fast** during the daytime and pray.

Nigerians also celebrate things like harvests and the change of seasons. In the south, the most important of these holidays is the Gelede Festival. It is held by the Yoruba people. It honors women and the earth. People dress up, wear masks, and dance.

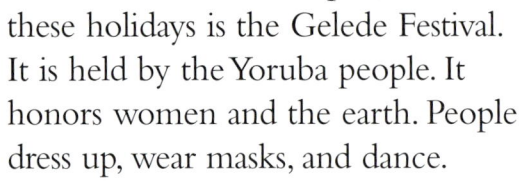

In the north, many people celebrate the Argungun Fishing Festival. This holiday marks the end of the growing season. People go to the Sokoto River to swim and play. There are also fishing and diving contests.

◀ **RAMADAN LANTERN**
Muslims fast and pray during the month-long holiday of Ramadan. They break the fast each night with a simple meal. They often eat by the light of traditional Ramadan lanterns.

LEARNING THE LANGUAGE

The three languages most widely spoken in Nigeria are Ibo, Hausa, and Yoruba. Below are some useful words and phrases in Ibo.

English	Ibo	How to say it
Good Morning	Ezigbo ututu	(AY-ZEE-BO oo-TOO-too)
Good Night	Ezigbo anyasi	(ay-zee-Bo-ahn-yeh-ah-see)
How are you?	Kedu	(kay-dooh)
I am fine	Odi Mma	(oh-dhee mee-ah)
Long time no see	Ote kwana	(oh-tah qua-nah)
Nice seeing you	Anya m jiu fu gi egbulam	(ahn-yeah me geeu foo gee ehboo-oo-lahm)

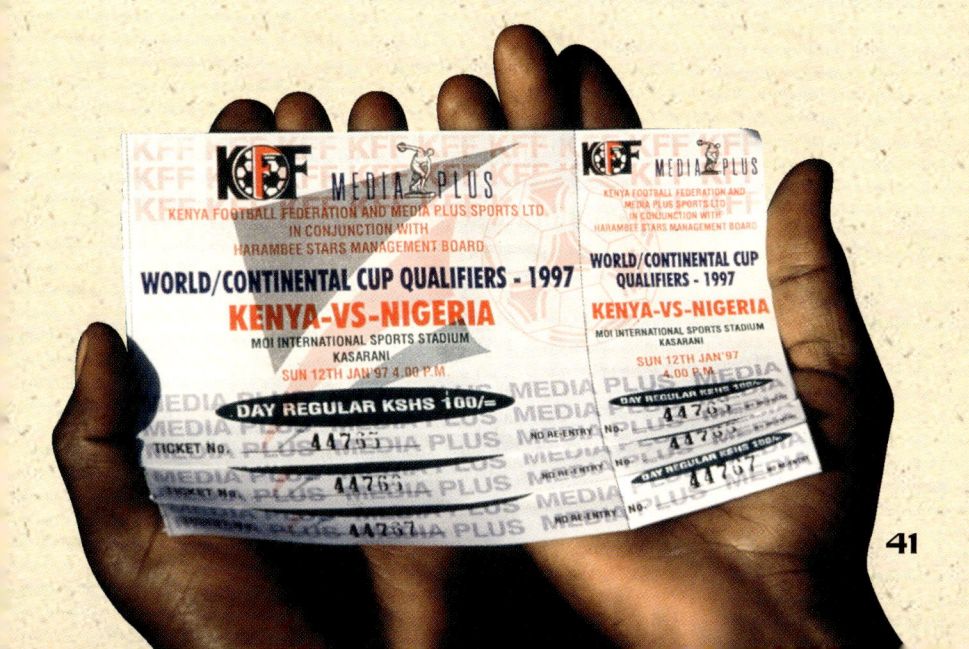

QUICK FACTS
NIGERIA

Capital ▶
Abuja

Borders
Niger (N)
Cameroon (E)
Gulf of Guinea (S)
Benin (W)

Area
356,667 square miles
(923,768 sq km)

Population
126,635,626

▼ **Main Religious Groups**

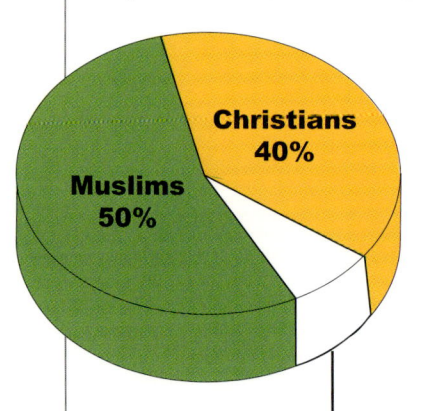

Christians 40%
Muslims 50%
Indigenous beliefs 10%

Largest Cities
Lagos (13,050,00)
Ibadan (1,365,000)
Ogbomosho (711,900)
Kano (657,300

Chief Crops
Peanuts, cocoa, palm oil, rubber, corn

Natural Resources
Crude oil, tin, columbite, iron ore, coal

▲ Flag of Nigeria

Coastline
530 miles (853 km)

Literacy Rate
51% of all Nigerians can read

Longest River ▶
Niger River
2,600 miles (4,180 km)

Major Industries
Food products, brewing, textiles, clothing

▼ **Monetary Unit**
Naira

43

PEOPLE TO KNOW

Many people have helped make Nigeria great. To find out who some of them are, check out the list below.

◀ WOLE SOYINCA

Wole Soyinka is famous around the world as a writer of novels, poetry, and plays. He won the Nobel Prize for his writing in 1986. This brought him widespread international attention. His most famous works include *The Road, A Play of Giants,* and *The Open Sore of a Continent.*

▶ HAKEEM OLAJUWON

Hakeem Olajuwon was born in Nigeria. Olajuwon eventually left Nigeria for the United States to play basketball. He is best known as a player with the Houston Rockets.

◀ SUZANNE WEGNER

Suzanne Wegner, an artist, has been living in the Sacred Forest for over 50 years. Originally from Europe, Wegner is devoted to restoring the Forest. She works to make sure that this art will last a long time. That way, many people will be able to enjoy it in years to come.

MORE TO READ

Want to know more about Nigeria? Check out the titles below.

Bailey, Donna. *Where We Live: Nigeria.* Austin, TX: Raintree Steck-Vaughn Publishers, 1992.

Tells about the every day life of Nigerian people, including the occupations, festivals, and ceremonies.

Berg, Elizabeth. *Nigeria (Festivals of the World).* Milwaukee, WI: Gareth Stevens Inc., 1998.

Describes how the culture of Nigeria is reflected in its many festivals, including the Argungu Fishing Festival and the Feast of Ogun.

Owhonda, John. *A Nation of Many People.* Parsippany, NJ: Silver Burdett Ginn, 1997.

Shows the geography, history, people, and culture of Nigeria. Includes a chapter on Nigerians in the United States.

Rambeck, Richard. *Hakeem Olajuwan.* Chanhassen, MN: Child's World Inc., 1995.

Describes the basketball career of Hakeem Olajuwon, who was born in Nigeria and is a star center on the Houston Rockets.

Rupert, Janet. *The African Mask.* Boston, MA: The Horn Book, Inc., 1994.

Set in Nigeria 900 years ago, this book tells the story of Layo, a 12 year-old Yoruba girl who wants to become a potter.

GLOSSARY

Antique (an-TEEK)—an old and rare object of value

Crop (KROP)—a plant grown in large amounts for food; wheat and corn are common crops

Currency (KUR-uhn-see)—the type of money used in a country

Current (KUR-uhnt)—something that is happening now and not in the past or future

Delta (DEL-tah)—a triangle-shaped area of land where a river deposits mud, sand, or pebbles as it enters the sea

Dense (DENSS)—very crowded or thick, like a thickly wooded forest

Embassies (EM-buh-sees)—the places or buildings in a country where ambassadors usually live and work

Execution (EK-suh-KYOO-shun)—the killing of someone who has committed a major crime

Fast (FAST)—to stop or give up eating food for a period of time

Free speech (FREE SPEECH)—to speak without being held back or told what to say

Inhabitants (in-HAB-it-tents)—a group that lives in a certain place or area

International (in-tur-NASH-uh-nuhl)—having to do with many different countries

Mineral Deposit (MIN-uh-ruhl di-POZ-it)—a natural layer of the ground that is neither plant nor animal; a layer of iron ore is an example of a mineral deposit

Metropolis (meh-TROP-uh-lis)—a major city that is the center of activity

Plain (PLANE)—a wide open space of land

Poverty (POV-ur-tee)—lacking wealth or being in a poor state

Rain Forest (RAYN FOR-ist)—a thick forest in the tropics where lots of rain falls

Sea level (SEE LEV-uhl)—a starting point determined by the average level of the ocean's surface, used to measure a place's height or depth

Shanties (SHAN-tees)—a simply made wooden hut or cabin

Shrine (SHRINE)—a building or monument that is considered sacred or holy

Swampland (SWAHMP-LAND)—a large area of marsh or wet, spongy ground that is usually not good for farming

Term (TURM)—the length of time an elected official is in office

Traditional Leader (truh-DISH-uh-nal LEED-ur)—a representative of the people who has inherited his title, like a king

INDEX

Abuja 32, 33, 42
animals 5, 22, 23, 29

batik fabric, dyes 18, 19, 20, 21
Benin 6, 9, 11
Brazilian Quarter 17, 19
British rule 7, 8, 9
bush taxis 20

Chad 6, 11
civil war 8, 9

Emir's Palace 20

Gashaka Gumpti
    National Park 22

harmattan 14, 15
Hausa 6, 7, 9, 28

Ibo 27, 28
Igbo 9
Ikoyi Island 18
Islam 21, 33, 40

Jos Plateau 4, 5, 6, 10

Kano 20, 21
kola nuts 30, 31

Lagos 16, 17, 26, 27
Lagos Island 16, 17
Lagos Mainland 18

mangrove 10
mosques 21, 33

naira (currency) 30, 43
National Museum 17, 19
National Theater 18, 19
Niger Delta 36, 37
Niger River 10, 12, 13
Nok civilization 6

Obasanjo, Olusegun 9, 38, 44
oil production 30, 36, 38, 39
Ojubo Oshun Shrine 25
Olajuwon, Hakeem 44

Port Harcourt 36, 37, 39

rain forests 10
Ramadan 40

Sacred Forest 24, 25, 33, 44
Sahara Desert 14, 15
sandstorms 15
savanna 10, 22
slavery, European 7
Soyinka, Wole 44

Victoria Island 17

water taxis 36, 37
Wegner, Suzanne 24, 44

Yoruba 6, 9, 24, 25, 28, 33, 44

48